D1426106

Welcome to the world of Beast Quest!

Tom was once an ordinary village boy, until he travelled to the City, met King Hugo and discovered his destiny. Now he is the Master of the Beasts, sworn to defend Avantia and its people against Evil. Tom draws on the might of the magical Golden Armour, and is protected by powerful tokens granted to him by the Good Beasts of Avantia. Together with his loyal companion Elenna, Tom is always ready to visit new lands and tackle the enemies of the realm.

While there's blood in his veins, Tom will never give up the Quest…

There are special gold coins to collect in this book. You will earn one coin for every chapter you read.

Find out what to do with your coins at the end of the book.

CONTENTS

For a time, I was the most powerful Master of the Beasts who ever walked this land. A royal prince. A courageous hero. People chanted my name.

But at the peak of my fame, it was taken from me by cowards.

For almost three centuries my spirit has wandered the realms. In ghostly form, I have searched for the one magical token that will bring me back.

And now I have found it, Avantia will pay for her treachery.

Only a fool would stand in my path.

Karadin

THE EAGLE'S NEST

Tom was glad to see Storm still waiting for them as he, Elenna and Silver finally reached the bottom of the mountain. Storm lifted his head and let out a whinny of greeting but Tom was so exhausted he could barely summon a smile in return. It had been a long climb down from the village of Colton. Elenna's face was pale, and covered in cuts and grazes. Tom had never seen her look so tired.

"Thank goodness we're back on level ground!" Elenna said. "I'd be happy to never see another mountain as long as I live."

"I'm with you on that!" Tom said.

Beyond the Grassy Plains, the rising sun cast a fiery glow along the horizon. The sight gave Tom little joy. It marked yet another night passed without sleep...another night where victory seemed further away than ever on what might be their hardest Quest yet.

As Tom reached Storm, the stallion nuzzled against him. Tom

gave his horse a quick rub and collapsed on to the nearest boulder. Elenna slumped down beside him and Silver stretched out at their feet, his flanks heaving. Tom felt a pang of guilt. The wolf had scouted ahead of them on their climb, and badly needed rest – but there was no time for that. Karadin, an ancient prince and former Master of the Beasts, had risen from the dead and was intent on taking Avantia's throne. His Evil ghost had already awoken two fearsome Beasts. Tom and Elenna had defeated them both, but Karadin had absorbed the creatures' magical essences and was now stronger than ever, while Tom's own powers were waning.

Elenna took a long drink from her water bottle then poured some into a natural dip in the rock for Silver.

"So, where do we go now?" she asked Tom.

"Back up into the mountains, I fear," a faint voice murmured from nearby. Shading his eyes against the glare of the rising sun, Tom could just make out the pale, shimmering outline of Loris, Karadin's ghostly brother. The spirit had been guiding Tom and Elenna on their Quest so far, but like Tom, Loris's strength was failing as Karadin's grew. He was now like clear ice in water, barely visible at all.

"You know where Karadin is headed next?" Tom asked.

Loris nodded. "He is making his way towards a lonely mountain peak called the Eagle's Nest. Long ago, Karadin defeated a griffin-Beast there. He will seek to raise Raptex once more."

Tom shook his head, frustration welling inside him. "If we defeat Raptex, Karadin will steal his powers and become stronger than ever! How can we hope to win?"

"There's always hope," Elenna said. "We can do this, Tom!" Despite her bowed shoulders and the dark hollows beneath her eyes, her words were fierce. They gave Tom heart.

"Elenna is right," Loris said. "You can still intercept Karadin before he awakens Raptex. The mountain paths are treacherous and always changing. They have become the final resting place of many unfortunate travellers. The way will not be easy, even for Karadin. You still have time."

Gazing back at the lofty heights they had just left, Elenna managed a weary smile. "Up once again it is, then…" she said. But then she glanced at Silver and her smile changed to an anxious frown. Tom noticed that the wolf's ribs showed under his shaggy coat, and he looked older than when they had left King Hugo's palace. Storm needed a proper rest and a good meal too.

"Let's take the animals as far as Colton," Tom said. "We can stable them there and pick up supplies for the rest of the journey. Though they may not know it, the villagers owe us a debt of thanks!" Tom and Elenna had recently saved the mountain village from flooding – not to mention the threat of the terrifying piranha-Beast Devora.

Loris bowed his head. "I must bid you farewell for now," he said. "My life force is almost spent, but I wish you luck." With those words, Loris's shimmering form became more translucent than ever, melting away. He soon vanished into the morning air.

Tom and Elenna set off at once, trudging back up the narrow mountain path with Storm and Silver behind them. The sun climbed higher in the blue sky as they travelled. It beat against Tom's shoulders and, coupled with an icy wind, meant he was soon both sweating and chilled to the bone.

By the time the squat stone

buildings of Colton came into sight, Tom's legs ached so much he could hardly move them, and hunger gnawed at his gut. A sudden whiff of roasting meat on the breeze made him quicken his pace.

As they neared the small town, he saw that bright awnings filled the village square.

"Market day!" Elenna said.

Tom nodded. "We're in luck. We should be able to get everything we need!"

After leaving Silver at the outskirts of town, Tom and Elenna led Storm up on to the rocky plateau that housed the village. But, to Tom's dismay, it soon became clear that

Colton had known better days. Most of the stalls had little produce on show – a few eggs, black bread and goats' milk. The villagers and stallholders looked thin and sallow, and shot Tom and Elenna wary glances as they passed. When Tom asked one woman if there was a stall selling maps of the peaks, she pulled her shawl close around her face and turned away without even answering.

"A simple 'no' would have been enough!" Elenna said, crossly.

"You're looking for a map?" a young boy asked. His freckled face was covered in grime but his blue eyes glinted with mischief. He was half carrying, half dragging a huge pail of milk and grinned broadly as he approached them, showing a gap between his two front teeth.

"Can you help us?" Tom asked him.

The boy shrugged. "Maybe," he said. "But not with a map. You can't make maps of the peaks. They're always changing, see? Avalanches block paths off and make big holes to fall down. Ten to one if you go up, you won't come back. You

need a guide – someone like me who knows the lay of the land. But I don't suppose you can afford one." The boy cocked his head and closed one eye appraisingly. Tom couldn't help smiling. The lad had to be no older than seven.

"Thanks for the offer, but I think I'll be all right," Tom said with a grin. He glanced about to check no one was watching, then took his yellow jewel from his belt. "This jewel helps me remember where I've been, so I won't get lost. And look…" He removed the purple jewel from its place and held it against the ground. The hard rock instantly disintegrated, leaving a small hole.

"Rock falls won't get in my way."

The boy's eyes widened. "I know who you are!" he said. "You're Tom, the Master of the Beasts!"

Tom smiled and nodded.

"That's right," Elenna said. "We just need provisions, and somewhere to stable our animals."

The boy's whole face lit up. "Well, in that case, you're in luck! My father's got the best stall in the market and a big stable you can use too. My name's Benji, by the way. Come with me!"

2

DECEIVED

Benji led Tom and Elenna to a
nearby stall selling skins of goats'
milk and wedges of cheese as
well as a few dry and wizened-
looking apples. A tall, sinewy man
with tattooed arms smiled as they
approached, showing a gap between
his teeth just like Benji's.

"Morning," the man said, nodding.

"It's not often we get travellers in these parts. I see you've met my son." Benji's father had broad, muscular shoulders, but beneath his stubble his cheeks were hollow and deeply lined. Behind him, a petite woman with long brown hair was cutting cheese with a length of wire.

"Put the milk over there, Benji," the woman said, gesturing to the bench behind her. Then she turned to Tom and Elenna, frowning in a way that made Tom only too aware of his grime-stained clothes. "What can we do for you?" she asked.

"Tom and Elenna need to stable their horse," Benji cut in before Tom could speak. "And they need provisions to go up into the mountains. They were after a map too, but I set them right about that – I told them I could be their guide." As Benji hefted his pail on to the bench, Tom untied his coin purse from his belt.

Benji's mother's gaze sharpened at once. "A stable's no problem," she said, smiling now. "We can provide bread and milk too, and maybe a bit of cheese and some apples. We've got ropes if you need them, and like Benji said, he can set you on the right path."

Tom nodded gratefully. *This is more like it!* he thought. *Finally, someone willing to help us.* "Thank you," he told Benji's mother. "That's just what we need."

Benji's father started filling skins with milk from the fresh pail while Benji wrapped bread and cheese in greaseproof paper, chattering away while he worked. Tom smiled as he heard the boy excitedly describing the jewels in his belt.

"Tom's the Master of the Beasts!" Benji boasted. "I recognised him and Elenna right away!"

"Well, I'll be...!" his father said. "Then they shall have the cream off the milk. Only the very best for our heroes!"

"We have another animal to house too," Elenna said. She turned and whistled through her fingers and a moment later, Silver bounded to her side.

Benji's mother took a step back, her eyes widening. "What type of dog would that be?" she asked.

"Wolf," Elenna said. "He'll be fine with water, meat and somewhere to sleep. Just don't try to tie him up."

The woman raised an eyebrow, then she sniffed. "Well, we can take him, but we'll have to charge extra. I'll get them settled now."

As Benji's mother led Storm away, Silver let out an anxious whine. Elenna pointed sternly.

"Go with Storm," she told her wolf. Silver did as he was told, but kept looking back over his shoulder until he was lost in the crowd.

Once the animals were gone, Benji's father handed Elenna and Tom each a skin of milk. Benji took one of his own, and after shouldering their packs, Tom and Elenna followed the boy through the village and upwards on to a winding mountain path.

Benji chattered constantly as they walked, telling Tom and Elenna about every traveller who'd passed through Colton, and the sticky ends they had come to.

"One man – I think he was called Roland – actually got crushed flat by a rock," the boy said. "Or that's what

Mother told me, anyway! She says you always have to keep your wits about you up here!"

"Sound advice," Elenna said.

Thinking of their recent battle against Devora the Death Fish in the lake above Colton, Tom couldn't agree more.

The path rose and fell, weaving between rocky outcrops and sharp ridges, dipping below overhangs and crossing deep ravines. In some places the way was so narrow Tom had to turn sideways and shuffle along the rock face, a sheer drop plunging away at his feet. Benji seemed unfazed and Elenna walked quickly and easily, but Tom's boots

barely fit on the path. He found himself holding his breath, willing himself not to look down. A pebble loosened by his passage tumbled away, bouncing off sharp outcrops as it fell. Tom swallowed hard, a sudden image of his own body making the same deadly journey flashing through his mind.

The air became colder and thinner and Tom began to feel light-headed. His leg muscles burned, and gusts of icy wind whipped tears into his eyes, blurring his vision. Elenna was panting as she climbed, her back bowed beneath her heavy pack and her cheeks flushed with exertion. Finally, they rounded a bend in the path and came to a sheltered plateau.

"I'm not allowed to go any further," Benji told them. "You should rest now too. The path is much steeper from here and there won't be anywhere to stop for ages." Tom sank gratefully to the ground and Elenna sat beside him. They both uncorked their skins of milk and drank. The cold, creamy liquid tasted wonderful, and instantly revived Tom a little. He took another swig while Elenna tipped her head back, gulping thirstily.

"There's still a long way to go to the Eagle's Nest," Benji told them between sips of his own drink. "There's tunnels and all sorts up ahead. People used to dig for gemstones up here. A few travellers still come, even though it's dangerous. One of the tunnels is said to be haunted by an explorer who was caught in a snowstorm. The mountain got covered in snow and ice, and no one found his body until the next spring... By then he was frozen solid, like a statue."

Listening to Benji chatter away, Tom suddenly felt strangely warm – *too* warm, and so sleepy he could barely keep his eyes open. He yawned, then shook his head to clear the woozy feeling, but his eyes blurred and he couldn't focus properly. He glanced at Elenna and saw she was swaying as if she might pass out. Benji had trailed off and was staring at them, frowning.

"Are you two all right?" the boy asked. "You both look...kind of sick."

Tom started to speak, but his tongue felt thick and clumsy, and he couldn't think of the words. When he tried to stand, his legs wouldn't obey him.

At his side, Elenna half rose, then crumpled forward on to the rock, out cold. *Elenna! No!* Suddenly a group of people appeared behind Benji, villagers from Colton, all carrying clubs and other makeshift weapons.

"No one needs to get hurt," a gruff voice said. Tom forced his eyes to focus and recognised Benji's father. "Hand over that belt of yours with all the jewels and we'll leave you be."

"Father! You can't!" Benji cried.

Tom looked at the flask in his hands, then back at the villagers. Suddenly everything made sense. *The milk's drugged. We've been betrayed!* Fury lent Tom a burst of energy. He called on the strength

of heart of his golden breastplate.
"No!" Tom managed, forcing himself
to his feet, staggering. "I need them
to defend the kingdom."

"And we need them so our families
don't starve," Benji's father said.

"I'll tell the king…you are in
need," Tom
said, his
speech
coming out
slurred. "He
will send aid.
But please,
let me…
keep my
belt." Tom
blinked

again. His world was spinning. He sank down on to his knees, sickness rising in his throat as the villagers surged forwards.

"Stop!" Tom shouted, his heart thumping with panic. Someone bent over him and tugged at his belt.

"Take that sword too!" another voice said. "We could get a few bob for that."

"Let them go!" Benji shouted. "They've not hurt us!" Nobody listened. Rough hands pulled and grabbed at Tom. He swiped with his fists but it was like moving through deep water. His vision kept swimming out of focus, and his lids were so heavy...

Tom heard a fierce growl and, as his eyes fell closed, he glimpsed sharp white teeth and amber eyes surging towards him.

KARADIN AGAIN

Tom groaned and rolled over, cradling his throbbing head with one hand as he pushed himself up to sitting. Blinking to focus, the first thing he saw was the mountainside plunging away in front of him... A wave of vertigo swept over him and he gagged, vomiting up sour, clotted milk. When his stomach was empty and the nausea settling, his memory flooded back. He felt for his belt... *No!* It was gone. But he still had his shield and his sword.

Already awake, Elenna sat with one arm draped around Silver's neck and her forehead resting against his thick grey fur.

"Are you all right?" Tom asked her.

"Not really," she croaked. "I feel like my brain is trying to escape."

"The villagers stole my belt," Tom told her. "I can't believe they tricked us! I feel like such an idiot for trusting them."

"Me too," Elenna said. "I guess it did all seem too good to be true.

Should we go after them?"

Tom thought for a moment. Losing his belt with the yellow jewel that would help him find his way out of the mountains was a blow. And he hated leaving Storm with people he couldn't trust. But when he considered turning around, the idea of leaving Karadin free to raise another Beast filled him with dread.

Tom let out a sigh. "No," he said. "Karadin already has a head start on us. We know where those villagers live. If they try to harm Storm, I'm pretty sure he'll make them wish they hadn't, and we can get my belt back later. For now, we have to press on."

They both heaved themselves up
and set off again. Silver kept close to
Elenna, his ears swivelling at every
sound and his hackles raised. The
sun had reached its high point while
they had lain unconscious, and
now it was making its slow descent
towards night. Tom did his best to
hurry, forcing his tired and aching
body to move faster, but as Benji had
warned, the mountain path quickly
became so steep that every step was
an effort.

Nausea washed over Tom in waves.
Elenna's face was grey and beaded
with sweat. Still, they kept going,
turning sharp corners, following
channels in the rock downwards,

then back up, only to find the way blocked by fallen stone.

Again and again they reached a dead end and traced their own steps back to be confronted with new terrain they had never seen before. Or worse, they would reach the end of a path that was completely unfamiliar, then realise they were back where they had started. *How is that possible?*

Tom growled as they reached yet another dead end. "Maybe we should make marks on the rock? Then at least we'll know we're not going in circles."

"It looks like you're not the first traveller to think of that," Elenna said, pointing at the sheer cliff face rising beside her. Tom could see what looked like arrows and dashes already scored on the stone.

He let out a heavy sigh, then etched a symbol of his own. They had no choice but to keep going, scoring lines at intervals to mark their passage as they went.

"Oh!" Elenna suddenly cried. Tom turned to see she had stopped and was gazing down a chimney-like hole in the mountain. He stepped to her side and looked down, then shuddered. Right at the bottom of the shaft lay the broken remains of a human skeleton grinning up at them, the dome of its yellowed skull

smashed
like an egg.

"Making
marks didn't
help him,"
Elenna said,
her voice
sounding
small and
lost.

Tom gently
took her shoulder and turned her
away from the horrible sight. "He
didn't have a friend and a wolf to
look after him," he said. "Let's go!"

Tom led the way, choosing his path
carefully, always trying to find the
quickest route up. With his marks

to keep them on track, they made better progress, and eventually the path became less twisted. The terrain opened out into a series of rocky summits separated by deep ravines, the last peak a needle-like point of rock so high its tip was lost in cloud.

"That must be the Eagle's Nest," Tom told Elenna, pointing. But when he turned, he saw her leaning against the rock face, her breathing laboured and her face as white as chalk.

"I need...to stop for a bit," she said, sitting down and resting her head on her knees. "What was in that milk? I still feel so sick..." Tom was starting to feel better, but he hadn't drunk nearly as much as Elenna. Silver nudged Elenna's cheek with his nose and let out an anxious whine.

"You stay here with Silver and recover for a while," Tom told Elenna. "I'll scout ahead and come back when I've worked out the best way to go."

Elenna nodded gratefully and closed her eyes. Tom set off again, knowing that Silver would keep Elenna safe. The path he followed led downwards at first, but then banked sharply up and through a narrow, steep-walled gorge. When Tom reached the top of the sloping channel, the view opened up once again, and this time the Eagle's Nest was right before him. With a clear view of their destination, his spirits lifted. But then he spotted a tall figure, dressed all in black, standing on a ledge about halfway up the jutting point. *Karadin!* The Evil ghost looked almost solid now, and was staring back the way they had come, towards the grassy plains. Even from this distance, Tom could see Karadin's face was etched with fury and hatred. Before Tom could hide, Karadin lowered his gaze, and his black, empty eyes locked with Tom's.

"Tell me, fine young hero," Karadin said, his voice seeming to speak right into Tom's ear. "Are you not tired of always trying to save the kingdom? You do look weary. And all the while King Hugo sits in luxury. Does he deserve that?"

Tom lifted his voice to shout back. "My reward is the safety of those I love. I have never asked my king for more than his gratitude."

"Can you really be so naive?" Karadin spat. "You have just had a taste of Colton's 'gratitude'. I will show you what Avantia's looks like!"

Karadin snapped his fingers and Tom felt an irresistible urge to turn and look out over the landscape, as if a powerful hand had caught hold of his chin and was forcing his gaze. He fought against it, but the magic was too strong. As Tom turned, a whooshing, rushing sensation filled his head. When he could see clearly again he was gazing at a busy, prosperous village from a bird's eye view. The sails of two huge windmills turned lazily above a bustling town square where a huge bronze statue stood. Plump, rosy-cheeked children and women wearing colourful dresses touched the statue as they passed it, as if for good luck. The statue itself was of a warrior, bearded and dressed in full armour with a spear in his hand and a shield at his side.

"Look at them!" Karadin snapped,

his voice loud and harsh. "The people of Millden practically worship my successor. Bard the Broad, they called him. Bard the Braggart, I say. He didn't even earn his title of Master of the Beasts.

My father just gave it to him – a
pretender from an unknown town
in the middle of nowhere. He got a
statue to mark his birthplace, too.
All I got was an unmarked grave in
the Gallery of Tombs. And one day,
you will rot there too, Tom. And no
one will care!"

With another rushing sensation
the vision dissolved into a blur of
bright colours. Tom felt as if he were
being dragged along on a strong
current, and blood pounded loud in
his ears. "Tell me, is that what you
want?" Karadin hissed. His voice
echoed right inside Tom's head,
making his skin crawl. "Or would
you rather learn to command the

Beasts as I do?" Karadin went on. "To take control of your destiny?" Tom felt a sudden terrible pressure about his throat. His eyes refocussed and he found himself gazing straight into Karadin's cruel black eyes. The Evil ghost was standing in front of him now, one skeletal hand fastened around his neck.

A DANGEROUS
CLIMB

Tom kicked out with all his strength
as Karadin lifted him off the ground
by the throat, crushing his windpipe,
squeezing the life from his body. Red
blotches swarmed in Tom's vision.
He kicked and thrashed but his
boots found no target. Tom suddenly
realised that, although Karadin's

x

skeleton hand was clamped tightly about his throat, the Evil prince's body had become spirit once more. *How can I fight an enemy that can turn into thin air at will?*

Darkness began to engulf Tom. His head felt as if it might explode from the pressure of the blood thundering inside it. *I'm going to die! This Quest will be my last. And I will have failed everyone...*

THUNK! Tom crashed to the ground holding his throat, coughing and wheezing as Karadin howled in agony. When the darkness cleared from Tom's vision he looked up to see the shaft of one of Elenna's arrows jutting from Karadin's arm, right where ghostly flesh joined bone. Elenna stood nearby with another missile already strung to her bow and Silver at her heels, growling fiercely.

"Step away from Tom!" she yelled.

Karadin backed away, his black eyes flashing with fury. The magical ring on his finger started to glow with a piercing white light.

As Tom scrambled to his feet, Karadin let out a triumphant cry and smashed his fist hard against the rock wall at his side. With a terrific splintering crack, the rock shattered apart and came tumbling down.

Tom leapt to Elenna's side, sheltering her and Silver behind his shield as debris thundered into

the gorge. Choking dust filled Tom's lungs and sharp chips of rock scoured against him. The terrible deluge went on and on... When the air finally cleared and all fell quiet, Tom lowered his shield. Karadin had gone and the way ahead was completely blocked by a towering wall of rubble.

Elenna ran her eyes up the colossal

pile and sighed. "Perfect! What should we do now?"

Tom was glad to see that under its layer of rock-dust her face had regained some of its normal colour. He smiled.

"First, I need to thank you for saving my life," he said. "Then, I suppose we'll have to climb. If I had my purple jewel, I could make a path through...but there's no point dwelling on that. I just hope Benji's father hasn't sold my belt to someone who can do real damage with it!"

Elenna put her hand on his arm. "As soon as we're done with Karadin we'll get it back," she said. Elenna bent to hug Silver. "Wait here," she told the wolf, who fixed her with his intense amber gaze. He clearly wasn't happy to be left, but he couldn't follow them where they were going.

Tom began the long climb up the rickety mountain of debris, wedging his fingers and toes into the gaps between sharp chunks of newly broken rock. Elenna began to scramble upwards too, further along the rock pile so that any rubble Tom dislodged wouldn't hit her on the way down. The rock cut deeply into Tom's sore palms each time he pulled himself higher and loose chunks shifted beneath his boots, making his heart shoot into his mouth. Sweat trickled down his face and into his eyes, making them sting. But finally, he and Elenna reached the top of the giant rock fall...only to find the sheer walls of the Eagle's Nest jutting up out of the rubble.

After taking just a moment to shake the tension from his arms and catch his breath, Tom started to climb once more. The rock here was stable, but there were hardly any cracks or ledges to grip, just smooth, vertical stone. Clinging with his fingers and toes, Tom spread his legs and arms wide like a spider, making use of every tiny hold. His leg and arm muscles soon shuddered with exertion and, from below, he could hear Elenna grunting as she pulled

herself up.
He longed
for a drink
of cold
water – even
a drop, but
he needed
both hands
to cling to
the cliff face.

Looking down at the jagged
ground far below made Tom's head
swim, so he kept his gaze firmly
turned to the climb left above.
Suddenly he spotted something – a
deep shadow that looked almost
like an opening in the cliff. And, as
he looked, Tom could see flickers

of ominous white light coming from deep inside. *Karadin is waking the Beast!* A desperate urgency took hold of him, giving him new strength and speed.

"Elenna, hurry! Head for that cave!" Tom called. Ignoring his screaming muscles, Tom pulled his aching body up the last stretch of sheer stone and finally scrambled into the opening. Looking down, he saw Elenna just below him and reached for her hand, using the power of his golden breastplate to pull her into the tunnel.

They both stood breathing heavily, staring into the shadows ahead. Another pulse of platinum light flared around them.

Tom broke into a run with Elenna pounding at his side. The passage soon opened out into a cavernous chamber filled from wall to wall with crystal shards. They stabbed down from the ceiling and jutted up from the floor, each as sharp as a dagger. And in the centre of the vast place stood Karadin. His ring glowed brightly, and as Tom watched a narrow beam of light shot from its stone and struck the ceiling above.

A kaleidoscope of dazzling light zigzagged around the rocky chamber and with a series of terrific crashes and crunches, the sharp crystal blades began to fall.

Dread twisted in Tom's gut as he realised that he was too late. In the cavern roof where the stalactites had been, he could now see the fossilised remains of a colossal Beast. And where the light from Karadin's ring struck the fossil, hard grey stone became feather and fur, muscle and sinew. A mighty Beast with the head and wings of an

eagle and the body of a lion pulled itself free of the rock. Tom gasped as the creature unfolded its vast wings and opened its eyes. They were a pure and blazing white, just like the magical light from Karadin's ring, and they were staring right at him...

THE RAGE OF RAPTEX

"Raptex will be the last Beast you ever face!" Karadin shouted, his taunt echoing around the chamber as the mighty griffin-Beast opened his beak and dived towards Tom and Elenna. Tom brandished his sword and Elenna aimed her bow but Raptex let out a screech so loud

it made the chamber quake. More
lethal shards of glittering crystal
rained down from the ceiling. Tom
pulled Elenna to him and raised his
shield above her. Stalactites crashed
against the wood as Raptex flapped

towards
daylight.

A shadow
streaked
past Tom
and Elenna,
following
the Beast.
Karadin! Tom
lunged after
the Evil
ghost, but at

the same moment Raptex shrieked again. Tom staggered, dropping his weapons and covering his ears as a blast of harsh, piercing sound drove through his skull like a pick. Elenna crouched, her head in her hands as the terrible cry echoed on and on, reverberating off the walls.

When the echoes finally died away, the chamber was dusky, the only light filtering in through a new wall of fallen crystal that blocked the cave mouth. The cavern floor glittered dimly with fallen shards and as Tom ran his eyes around the rock walls, he saw there were no other tunnels or entrances. *No escape.*

Elenna looked at him, her jaw clenched and her expression fierce. "I am not dying like one of the travellers in Benji's stories. I am going to get us out of here!" She picked up a sharp spike of crystal and swung it at the blockade. Her blow didn't leave a trace.

Tom hacked at the pile of broken shards with his sword, but the stuff was almost as hard as diamond, and wedged in tight. Even calling on the strength of his golden breastplate and the sword skills of his golden gauntlets combined, he only managed to chip the gleaming stone.

Frustration raged inside him. "We're trapped, and Karadin could

be doing anything!" he cried. He
pulled his arm back to strike at the
crystal again, but Elenna grabbed
his wrist.

"Shhh!" she said. Tom was about
to protest – they had to get out! But
then Elenna put a finger to her lips,
and pointed to the crystal blocking
the cavern entrance. Tom's scalp
prickled as he heard something.
A deep rumbling sound, getting
steadily louder by the moment,
rising to a crunching, churning roar.
Is the Beast returning?

"Get back!" Tom shouted, lifting
his shield and holding it before
them both, just as a terrific *boom!*
filled the cave. A glittering cloud

of dust rolled over Tom and he felt
the heavy thud of debris hitting his
shield. When the dust settled and he
let his shield fall, he saw the tunnel
entrance was once again clear.
And grinning back at him from
the other side, holding a glowing
purple jewel, was Benji. Silver stood

at Benji's side, his tongue lolling happily. Elenna dropped to one knee and Silver bounded towards her and started licking her face and hands.

"Here," Benji said, slotting the purple jewel into place and handing Tom his belt.

"Thank you!" Tom said, relieved to have all his magical tokens back. "How did you find us?" he asked Benji.

"Storm kept snorting and neighing to be let out of the stable," Benji said. "I figured he wanted to come to you. So, seeing as I thought what Mother and Father did was pretty shabby, I decided to put things right. I stole your belt back, and rode

Storm after you. I left Storm by the lake because of the climbing, and after that I found Silver. He led me to the Eagle's Nest and started pawing at the rock, so I guessed you were trapped. I remembered what you said about your purple jewel. And the rest is history!"

Benji was grinning so hard, Tom couldn't help doing the same. He patted the boy on the back.

"You did brilliantly!" Tom said.

"Although I'd like to know what was in that milk," Elenna added, crossly.

Benji put up his hands. "I knew nothing about that!" he said. "And please don't be too hard on Father. He works all the hours. And I know Mother tries to hide it, but she misses meals sometimes so I get enough to eat. They were just doing what they thought they had to."

"Hmm," Elenna said. "I still don't think poisoning people is the answer. But I'm sure King Hugo will send supplies once he knows how hard things are in Colton. In the meantime, we have a Beast to defeat." Elenna turned to Tom. "Do you have any idea where Karadin will have gone?"

Tom thought of the ghost prince's crazy ranting, and the vision he'd forced on Tom. He nodded. Karadin had a score to settle.

"He'll be heading for a town called Millden."

THE GRASSY PLAINS

Now that Tom was equipped with his purple jewel, and they had Silver and Benji to lead the way, getting out of the mountains proved far quicker than getting up had been. Still, dread churned in Tom's gut each time he thought of the griffin-Beast Karadin had awoken.

With Raptex to carry him, Karadin would reach Millden in no time at all!

The afternoon sun was beginning to fade as Tom and his companions made it to the lake above Colton. Storm snorted and whinnied joyfully when he spotted them, and Tom was glad to see his horse looked rested and well groomed.

"Thank you for your help!" Tom told Benji. "We would still be trapped in a cave if it weren't for your quick thinking."

"And now you'll have a tale to tell about two travellers who *did* make it out of those mountains alive," Elenna added with a grin. "You'll be the story's hero!"

Benji smiled back. "No one would ever believe it."

"They might if they see this," Elenna said, holding out a small chunk of crystal she had collected from Raptex's cave. "And you can take one of my arrowheads too, as a thank you!" Elenna selected a shiny black one from the pouch she carried and gave it to Benji.

Benji's face glowed with pride and pleasure as

he held the two tokens. "I'll never forget meeting you," he told Tom and Elenna. "Maybe one day I could be a Master of the Beasts too," he added.

Tom smiled. "You are brave and you are honest. I think you have just what it takes!"

Tom leapt up on to Storm's back, and Elenna swung up behind him. After one final wave to Benji, they set off for the Grassy Plains with Silver running at Storm's side.

The stallion was soon cantering smoothly over the rolling grassland, but long before they reached Millden Tom heard the chilling sound of Raptex's hideous screech echoing over the plains. He urged Storm to an even faster gallop.

As the village came into view, Raptex's terrible screeching was joined by thuds and screams that made Tom's chest tighten with horror. Above the rooftops he could see Karadin riding on Raptex's back. The Beast swooped low, tearing huge swathes of cloth from the sails of one of the town's windmills. Then he dived to snatch the thatching from a roof, and tossed it down into the streets below.

Fury welled in Tom's chest. "While there is blood in my veins, Karadin will be stopped!"

Following Raptex's trail of
destruction, Tom rode Storm
onwards through deserted streets
scattered with debris, and into the
square at the heart of the village.
Raptex was swooping back and

forth above the square with Karadin on his back. Market stalls had been thrown over and fallen produce lay in the gutters. Each time the Beast screamed, the windows rattled and the few townsfolk who had not already found shelter cowered with their hands over their ears.

Tom watched in horror as the Beast's glowing gaze fixed on a woman with three small children huddling beside an overturned cart. Frozen with terror, the mother pulled her children closer to her and closed her eyes.

"Revenge is mine!" Karadin shrieked as Raptex dived towards his innocent victims, brandishing his huge curved claws.

Elenna slid from Storm's back and aimed an arrow at the Beast while Tom dug his heels into his stallion's sides. Elenna let her arrow fly. It whizzed through the air and slammed into Raptex's broad wing, but the Beast didn't even register the strike. Elenna fired again, her arrow lodging deep in the flesh of Raptex's muscled flank. Again, the Beast flew on, undaunted. Tom drew back his sword as Storm thundered towards the cart. Raptex swooped low, his sharp claws reaching for the woman and children, who screamed and clung tightly to each other.

"Back!" Tom roared, swinging his

blade for Raptex's leg and slicing the flesh as he cantered past. With a deafening screech, Raptex wheeled around to face Tom. *At least he felt that!*

"Run!" Tom called to the terrified family. They stared at him, open-mouthed, too frightened to move. Elenna raced towards them, grabbed the two older children by the hand and pulled them up. The mother followed Elenna, carrying her last child to safety.

Tom put his hand to the red jewel in his belt and locked eyes with the Beast.

"Leave this place!" he told Raptex as the griffin's huge wings beat the air in front of him. "Karadin is not your master. You do not have to obey his commands!"

"You are the one that must leave!" Karadin screamed from Raptex's back. "I am the Master of the Beasts now. Raptex!" Karadin commanded. "Lay waste to this wretched place. And start with *that*!" He extended a hand and pointed to the statue that loomed over the square.

"No!" Tom commanded. "Do not listen to him!" But Raptex's head had swivelled around and his glowing white eyes were fixed on the bronze figure of Bard. With another piercing shriek that forced Tom to cover his ears, the

Beast dived. Raptex lashed at the metal as he swooped past, raking it with his giant claws. Sparks flew, but the statue didn't tremble.

"Again!" Karadin roared, tugging on the Beast's shaggy pelt, bringing him around for another attack.

Turning Storm, Tom drew his own weapon, but then saw something that filled him with dread. A group of villagers had taken up scythes and threshing sticks and were making their way towards Bard's statue, ready to defend their town. The villagers, men and women, young and old, threw themselves in front of the bronze statue, their weapons raised, ready to meet Raptex's attack. But Tom had seen how little impact Elenna's arrows had had on the Beast. As Raptex shifted his gaze from the bronze statue to the innocent people surrounding it, Karadin's lips spread into a smile that chilled Tom to the core.

A DESPERATE CHALLENGE

As Storm galloped towards the
statue and the townsfolk defending
it, Tom called on the power of his
golden boots. Then, with his eyes
on Raptex, Tom pulled his horse
to a sudden halt, throwing himself
out of the saddle towards the Beast.
Storm's momentum combined with

the magical
power of
his boots
propelled Tom
through
the air. He
slammed hard
into Raptex's
flank, driving
the Beast off
course just
before he reached the villagers.
Winded and bruised, Tom hurtled
onwards, somehow managing to dip
his head and tuck into a roll as he
hit the flagstones…

Pain exploded in his shoulder and
his teeth clashed together, but he

scrambled up to see Raptex land in the square. The Beast seemed bigger than ever, huge muscles rippling beneath the gold pelt of his lion's coat and great wings spread wide. The Beast's claws, each as long as Tom's hand, glinted like volcanic glass and his hooked beak curved to a serrated point made to rend and tear flesh. Tom's sword felt small in his hand, measured against such a creature. But then he had a thought. *Raptex is not my enemy! Karadin is.* It gave Tom an idea. He stood straight and lifted his sword, looking Karadin firmly in the eye.

Karadin scowled at him from Raptex's back. "You are wasting my time, boy!" Karadin spat. "No one can stop me fulfilling my rightful destiny now!"

Tom shrugged. "If that is the case, you won't be afraid of a fair challenge. Man against man, Master of the Beasts against Master of the Beasts."

"You are no man!" Karadin shouted. "And you are no Master of the Beasts either!"

"In that case, your victory is assured," Tom said calmly. "I challenge you to a duel!"

Karadin leapt from Raptex's back. "Stay out of the way!" he barked at the Beast. Then he turned and swept his gaze around the villagers who had gathered in the square. "Someone give me a weapon!"

A stooped and elderly man with a red-grey beard tossed an axe down before the Evil ghost, who snatched it up, then turned to face Tom once more.

Karadin was a head taller than Tom, and muscular. He hefted the weapon confidently, swung it a few times, and smiled again. "This shouldn't take long…" Karadin said.

Running his gaze over his opponent, and remembering Karadin's hand squeezing his throat, Tom wondered if he had made a mistake. *He can turn into shadow to evade my blows…so what is his weakness?* Suddenly Tom had it. *Vanity!*

Tom turned to the statue of Bard and dropped to one knee, bowing his head. "I dedicate this battle to Bard the Broad and to all the true, valiant Masters of the Beasts who have come before me," Tom proclaimed. When he stood again, Tom saw Karadin's jaw working with fury, his face darkening. Tom smiled. *It's working...*

But Karadin looked at the axe in his hand, then back at Tom, an expression of utter disdain on his face. He shook his head. "What am I doing?" Karadin said, speaking almost to himself. "I don't need to prove anything to anyone. I am Avantia's rightful king!" Karadin turned back to the Beast waiting still and silent behind him.

"Destroy this village," Karadin shrieked. "Bring down the statue! I don't want anyone left alive! And you can start by killing the boy!"

KARADIN'S VOW

Raptex fixed his eyes on Tom and rose into the air, buffeting the square with a fierce wind. Some of the villagers stood their ground and raised their weapons. Others screamed and fled. Tom sank into a fighting stance and raised his sword as Raptex brandished his massive claws. *If Karadin won't fight, I have*

no choice but to defeat the Beast!

Raptex let out an ear-piercing shriek and dived. Tom stood tall despite the hideous pain driving through his skull. He waited for just the right moment, hoping to aim a clean strike at the creature's chest... But Raptex banked sharply before he reached Tom, aiming instead for the statue of Bard. With a mighty *crash!* Raptex slammed both forefeet into the bronze. Tom gulped in horror as the giant statue toppled towards him, filling his view. He lifted his shield and leapt sideways, trying to get out of the way, but it was too late. *OOF!* The statue smashed into Tom's shield, buckling

his arm and
driving him
to the ground
gasping with
pain. The
colossal weight
forced him
lower, crushing
the air out of
him, pinning
him in place.

Tom tried to move, but it seemed
that the only thing between him and
slow, painful death was his shield.
He was trapped. Helpless.

No! I will not die like this!
Summoning the strength of his
golden breastplate and tensing

every sinew of muscle in his body, Tom let out a terrific roar and shoved the statue away. But as soon as he was free of the crushing weight, he saw Raptex's claws swiping for his head. He rolled away, panting and gasping.

"Tom! Keep him busy just a bit longer!" Elenna cried. "I have a plan." Glancing towards her, Tom saw Elenna swing up on to Storm's back and canter away. Before he could even wonder what she had in mind, Raptex's sharp, serrated beak slashed for his chest.

Tom rolled again and leapt up, then broke into a limping run, trying to put space between himself and the Beast. Raptex leapt into the air, swooped over Tom's head and landed in front of him. The Beast's eyes glowed as bright as ever. Apart from the line of dried blood from the cut on his leg, he was uninjured. While Tom was bruised and battered all over, Raptex looked as fresh as when he had first awoken.

"Hurry up and finish him!" Karadin shouted.

Silver let out a fierce growl and leapt to Tom's side. Gratitude welled inside Tom. But he knew neither he nor the wolf were a match for this Beast. Silver pounced, teeth bared, snapping for the griffin's throat. Raptex batted the wolf from the air in mid-flight, slamming him sideways like an annoying fly.

"No!" Tom heard Elenna scream at the same time as he registered Storm's hoofbeats. He glanced over to see Elenna riding the stallion at full speed into the square, trailing a great swathe of white fabric – the torn sail from a windmill. Raptex turned at the sound of Elenna's cry too, and lunged towards her, but Elenna was ready. She lifted the fabric high and swept it over the Beast's head.

"Now!" she screamed at Tom. "Strike now!" Raptex squawked and thrashed, turning his head this way and that, blinded by the cloth. Tom lifted his sword, but then saw something else – Bard's huge, bronze spear, shining on the ground. He hefted the massive weapon up and hurled it with all the magical

strength of his breastplate towards the Beast. The missile drove through the Beast's wing, pinning it to the ground. Raptex thrashed harder, yanking at his wing, shaking his head and scrabbling at the earth with his claws. But he couldn't free himself. At last, he sank to the ground, flanks heaving.

Tom put one hand to the red jewel in his belt. *I told you, I am the true Master of the Beasts*, he told Raptex. *You have felt the blade of my sword once. I do not wish to use it again. Do you yield?*

I...yield... The Beast's voice echoed in his mind, raspy and harsh now, rather than piercing.

"No!" Karadin howled. "Get up, you stupid bird! You can't just lie there! I am your master."

Tom turned his sword on the prince. "He submits," Tom told Karadin. "And you should do the same."

"Never!" Karadin roared, raising his hand. "I will conquer this kingdom." The ring on Karadin's finger sent out a searing flare of brilliant white light. Blinded, Tom lunged, swinging his sword for the last place he had seen Karadin's form. But his blade found empty space, and when the light faded and Tom's vision returned, the ghost was gone. Tom turned at

once to Raptex, half knowing
what he would find. His fears were
instantly confirmed. The Beast lay
still, frozen in time, a grey fossil
once more. His essence was gone –
stolen by Karadin just as Devora's
and Gorog's had been. Tom felt a
pang of sorrow for the creature, but
turned his attention to the living.
Elenna stooped over Silver, who was
rising, shaking his head groggily.

"You're all right!" Elenna said,
hugging her wolf. She lifted
shimmering eyes to Tom. "I thought
that brute had killed him!"

"No, you made sure of that," Tom
said. "That was quick thinking to
use the sail!"

"You did some quick thinking yourself," Elenna said, smiling. "Thank goodness for Bard the Broad and his spear!" Suddenly Elenna's smile faltered. "Still, we are no better off than we were before," she said. "Worse, in fact. Now Karadin has the power of three Beasts at his disposal."

Tom nodded slowly. He was exhausted and battered. This had to be their toughest Quest yet. And Karadin was still at large, with more power than ever. But Tom was alive, as were Elenna, Silver and Storm. Beyond Elenna, Tom could already see the people of Millden emerging from their hiding places and staring in wonder at Raptex's statue-like form.

"No innocent lives have been lost," Tom told Elenna. "The villagers can rebuild their town. For now, I'll take that as a win! And while there's blood in my veins and I have my friends at my side, Karadin will never succeed."

THE END

CONGRATULATIONS, YOU HAVE COMPLETED THIS QUEST!

At the end of each chapter you were awarded a special gold coin. The QUEST in this book was worth an amazing 8 coins.

Look at the Beast Quest totem picture opposite to see how far you've come in your journey to become

MASTER OF THE BEASTS.

The more books you read, the more coins you will collect!

Do you want your own Beast Quest Totem?

1. Cut out and collect the coin below
2. Go to the Beast Quest website
3. Download and print out your totem
4. Add your coin to the totem

www.beastquest.co.uk

READ THE BOOKS, COLLECT THE COINS!
EARN COINS FOR EVERY CHAPTER YOU READ!

550+ COINS
MASTER OF
THE BEASTS

410 COINS
HERO

350 COINS
WARRIOR

230 COINS
KNIGHT

180 COINS
SQUIRE

44 COINS
PAGE

8 COINS
APPRENTICE

READ ALL THE BOOKS IN SERIES 27:
THE GHOST OF KARADIN!

Don't miss the next exciting Beast Quest book: GARGANTUA THE SILENT ASSASSIN!

Read on for a sneak peek...

THE SERPENT OF STONEWIN

"What a mess!" Elenna said as she and Tom made their way through the dim, deserted streets of Millden towards the village stables. "I wish we could help the villagers rebuild."

Tom squinted through the gloom,

running his eyes over the destruction left by their battle with Raptex. Broken windows, smashed by the griffin-Beast's deafening cry, stared darkly back at him from either side of the street. Some of the buildings were little more than empty husks with splintered timbers poking through holes in their roofs and walls.

Tom shook his head at the devastation. "We'll ask King Hugo to send aid when we get back to the palace," he said.

He and Elenna were on a Quest to prevent the Evil ghost-prince Karadin from stealing Avantia's throne. Karadin had once been

Master of the Beasts, and since rising from the grave he had already awakened three terrible creatures. Tom and Elenna had defeated each one in turn, but Karadin had absorbed the Beasts' magical essences and was now stronger than ever, while Tom's own powers were failing fast.

Glancing up, he noticed the first grey streaks of dawn light were already creeping into the sky. His stomach clenched with dread. "We'd better hurry!" he said.

As they reached the stables, Tom shouldered the door open and he and Elenna pushed through into the warmth inside. Tom's stallion Storm tossed his head, whinnying softly; Silver, Elenna's wolf, yawned and got stiffly to his feet.

"I know," Elenna said gently, running a hand through his thick coat. "It's far too early!"

While Tom saddled Storm, Elenna packed away the bread and fruit they had been given by the villagers. As he tightened the final buckle, Tom heard the soft clearing of a throat. He turned and made out the faint, shimmering outline of Karadin's younger brother, Prince Loris. The ghost was tall and broad, with the bearing of a man still in his youth. Tom felt a surge of pity. Loris had guided them on their Quest so far, but, like Tom, his strength was waning as Karadin's grew. Now only his sorrowful eyes were clearly visible.

"Loris," Tom said, bowing his head in greeting. "Do you know where Karadin is heading next?"

"My brother will make his way to Stonewin Volcano," Loris said. His voice was barely more than a sigh, and Tom had to lean in close to hear him. "Karadin will do all in his power to awaken the terrible Beast who lies there."

"That's Epos's home," Elenna said.

Loris nodded. "But Epos is not the only Beast of Stonewin. Long ago, my brother and I travelled there to face the mighty serpent Gargantua. We became separated…" A grimace of pain flitted across Loris's pale, translucent features. "It was my final battle. Watch…"

Loris spread his hands as if opening a book. At the same moment, Tom's vision blurred, and the stable floor seemed to drop away beneath his feet. He staggered, trying to find his balance as a sudden glare of bright sunlight blinded him. Focussing his eyes, Tom found himself standing on a high mountain ledge, staring into the mouth of a cave. A strong wind swirled around him, and from deep inside the cave ahead he could hear the muffled clashes and bangs of a battle, along with the furious hiss of a Beast.

Tom tried to lunge towards the cave, to add his strength to the fight, but he couldn't move. His body wasn't his own. Just then the loudest hiss yet echoed from the darkness, followed by a man's anguished cry, cut short...

Loris spoke into the sudden quiet. "I feared my brother was dead," he said. "I was wrong."

In the vision, Karadin burst from the cave. His cloak was torn, and he held a bloodied sword aloft, but he appeared unhurt – and young. The prince's eyes were a clear, bright blue instead of the black holes of the ghost-prince Tom had met on this Quest. Something on Karadin's finger caught the light of the sun –

something Tom recognised: a silver ring in the shape of a snake eating its own tail. It bore a single clear stone that shone like a star.

"I had never seen the ring before that day," Loris said. "I should have known what it meant…"

Tom saw the awful moment unfold: as Loris turned, Karadin lunged, thrusting his sword deep into his brother's mortal flesh.

Beside Tom, Elenna gasped in horror, and the vision dissolved into ripples of colour like driving rain on a pane of glass. When Tom could see again, he was standing in the dim stable once more. Silence briefly fell as the shock of the murder sank in.

Read
GARGANTUA THE SILENT ASSASSIN
to find out what happens next!

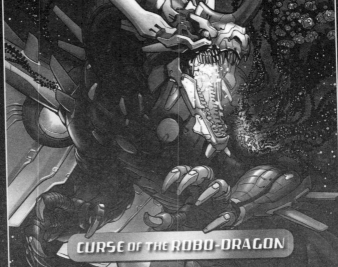